Slumgullion
The Executive Pig

A tale told in rhyme
Of a swine in his prime

Written by Matt S. Cibula

Illustrated by Tamara L. Boudreau

Zino Press
CHILDREN'S BOOKS

Middleton, Wisconsin

CHILDREN'S BOOKS

A Division of Knowledge Unlimited, Inc.

2348 Pinehurst Drive
Middleton, WI 53562
800 356-2303

SLUMGULLION, THE EXECUTIVE PIG
Text © 1994 by Matt S. Cibula
Illustrations © 1994 by Zino Press Children's Books
Illustrations by Tamara L. Boudreau
Designed by Maggie Zoeller
Printed in the U.S.A.

ISBN 1-55933-149-6

Library of Congress Catalog Card Number 94-60433

*To Liza, Mom, Dad, Tim, Jeff, Judith,
the students of Crossroads School and
Murray Language Academy, and all kids
everywhere, even the old ones.*

Slumgullion Pyg,
Who grew up on a farm,
Is the star of this rhyme.
He suffered no harm
As he fed upon fig
After fig after fig
In the bright summertime.
And he felt no alarm
As he got mighty big
In the leg and the arm
And he rolled in the slime,
The mud and the slime.

His friend Mr. Jones
Always smiled with concern
As he stroked Slummy's skin
(Rather pink with sunburn).
Jones spoke in sweet tones,
Fed Slummy ice-cream cones,
And said with a grin,
"Eat and earn, eat and earn!
This flesh on your bones
Gives me money to burn!
So open that chin
And put more food in!"

Slummy found these words odd,
Strange, unnerving and weird,
So he turned on his brain
And his memory cleared:
His old Grand-uncle Todd
And his mean Cousin Maude
In whose wallows he'd lain—
They'd both disappeared!
And so had his friend Claude!
Slummy's mother, who'd reared
Him and kept him from pain,
Wasn't there to explain.

For she'd just left one day
And not come back again.
But she'd said, "Always know
Pigs should never trust men.
That big barn painted grey
Is where they'll make me stay.
Mr. Jones is your foe.
I'll come back to the pen
When I can find a way.
Please stay slim until then,
'Cause if he makes you grow —
Run away, and not slow."

*S*lummy knew fear at last.
He looked up from his lunch
And he thought for a while.
Then he stopped in mid-munch —
And he ran away. Fast
As a lightning-bolt blast,
Slummy flew for a mile
Because he had a hunch
And a fear unsurpassed
That big pigs in Jones' bunch
Earned Jones' biggest smile
For a purpose most vile.

*W*hen he got to the fence
He looked back, breathing hard—
Then he thought of his mum
And slipped out of the yard.
For although he was tense,
Slummy knew self-defense.
His heart beat like a drum
And he moved on his guard
Till, a hundred yards hence,
A nice man named Bernard
Called out, "Hey! Yo! Chum!
Can I help? You look glum!"

Slumgullion said,
"Please, can I have a ride
To Zaire, or Mount Brown,
Or where'er I could hide?
If I go home instead
I may end up dead."
Bernie frowned out a frown,
Saying, "Pig, get inside.
Jones is sick in the head
And I don't want you fried.
We must get out of town
Before it's sundown."

"You'll need clothes for this scene
Or things will get drastic,
'Cause nude, you're a nerd."
Bernie took out some plastic
And bought shirts in green,
Shoes aquamarine,
Purple jackets absurd,
Paisley ties quite fantastic,
Striped trousers cut clean,
Suspenders elastic —
Slummy smiled like a bird
Who'd just said his first word.

When they left the clothes store
Bernie turned with a jerk
And said, "Now all you need
Is some help finding work."
The well-dressed young boar
Asked, "Me? Work? What for?"
Bernie answered with speed,
"You'll go quite berserk
With no job. Mop a floor!
Drive a truck! Be a clerk!
But before we proceed,
We must teach you to read."

"For reading's not tough.
I'll teach you real quick,"
Bernie said. And he did.
Slummy learned every trick,
From the real easy stuff
To words rougher than rough.
His friend then said, "Kid,
Now a job you must pick.
And no job is fluff
If you know that you're slick.
So don't flip your lid."
Slummy did as was bid.

He tried every try
And searched every search
And called every call
But got left in the lurch.
Slummy sighed with a sigh,
"Why me, Bernie? Why?"
"Kid, you can't win 'em all.
Just don't budge from your perch.
They might make you cry
But stand straight, like a birch,
And, like a birch, tall!
You're tough, you won't fall."

Slummy tried not to sink.
He stood tall in his shoes,
But he got pretty tired
Of hearing bad news.
Then he went to Fink, Inc.
In an office all pink

FINK INC.

He heard, "Johnson, you're fired!
Take a walk! Take a cruise!"
Slummy saw Mr. Fink:
"Hire me! You won't lose!"
Slummy's spunk Fink admired,
So Fink said, "You're hired!"

It was so hard at first
Being Vice-President,
For the problems they came
And not too many went.
But our friend never cursed
His fate as the worst,
And he earned a good name
'Cause he said what he meant
And his hopes never burst
And his dreams never bent.
Work was fun, like a game
Called "Money and Fame."

Mr. Fink was impressed
With his new employee
And he loved to write
All the traits he could see:
"Hard-working," "Well-dressed,"
"Handles any request."
But these words caused fright
In Gayle, Dave and Bea;
They feared all the rest,
So they feared Slummy P.
They plotted each night
With hearts full of spite.

One day Dave stayed late
To sneak and to snoop,
And noticed a tail.
He knew he had a scoop
That just couldn't wait
And rushed, feeling great,
Right home to call Gayle,
The head of the group.
Gayle laughed, full of hate,
And whooped with a whoop,
"We'll make Slummy fail
By telling his tale!"

So Gayle made her report.
The next day, Slummy thought
Something didn't quite fit,
But he knew he'd been caught
When old Mr. LaPort
Said, "Hey, Piggy! Snort! Snort!"
Then Bea, the nit-wit,
Sneered, "We found out your plot.
You're not quite our sort
Because human you're not.
I'm so mad I could spit!
You're a pig! Admit it!"

"**S**o what if I am?"
Slummy said with no pout,
"I'm a pig, but not scared,
'Cause myself I don't doubt.
I won't quit, I won't scram.
I'd rather be a canned ham!!"
But the others all stared
And they all whirled about —
Fink was standing — KA-BLAM —
With his chin all thrust out;
He seemed well-prepared
And he said, like he cared:

"**I** have heard the whole story
From beginning until now.
Slummy, a hog?
I don't care anyhow.
Fire him? Negatory!
He should only get glory.
He fits like a cog.
Him I would allow
In my territory
Whether sturgeon or cow.
And don't fall off your log,
But, my friends, I'm a dog!"

Fink shed his man-suit
And he gave a good shake,
Which prompted another
To say, "I'm a snake!"
And, with a salute,
Gave <u>his</u> suit the boot.
A croak came from a brother
Who called himself Jake.
Here an owl gave a hoot —
Here a duck — there a drake —
Then, a voice like no other:
Could it be?

     Slummy's mother?

"Oh, Mom!" he yelled loud,
All enwrapped in a hug,
"Could it really be true?"
Then they fell on the rug.
"Is this really allowed?"
She yelled over the crowd,
"After all we've been through,
To hold you so snug?
Slummy, I'm so proud!
That Jones was a thug.
I knew, I just knew
He'd never get you."

"I got a job here
And was saving my money
So I could come back
And pick you up, honey,"
Mommy said through a tear.
Then Fink sent up a cheer:
"To Slummy! Each yak,
Kookaburra and bunny
Must no longer fear
Being thought of as funny!
Be yourself! Quack a quack!
Slummy's shown us the knack!"

hen the crowd turned to Dave
And his two nasty friends;
The three smiled at the throng
As if to make amends,
But nobody gave
A smile or a wave.
So they ran before long,
For a bad human tends
To be not so brave
When his power ends.
And right over wrong
Always ends in a song:

"Fink barks and Jake croaks
In our workplace bizarre;
Fink, Inc., is the place
Where the animals are.
We play and we coax
Other animal folks
To wear their own face
And to be their own star —
For it isn't a hoax
And it's not very far
To where we embrace
With animal grace."